SCOOBY-DOO! and YOU:

A Collect the Clues Mystery

THE CASE OF THE LIVING DOLL

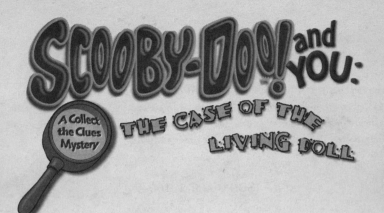

SCOOBY-DOO! and YOU:
A Collect the Clues Mystery
THE CASE OF THE LIVING DOLL

By Tracy West

WORLDWIDE PUBLISHING™

SCHOLASTIC INC.

New York   Toronto   London   Auckland   Sydney
Mexico City   New Delhi   Hong Kong

ISBN 0-439-23160-4

12 11 10 9 8 7 6 5 4 3 2 1   1 2 3 4 5 6/0

Cover and interior illustrations by Duendes del Sur
Cover and interior design by Madalina Stefan

Printed in the U.S.A.

First Scholastic printing, April 2001

You zip along the sidewalks of New York City on your scooter. It's a sunny day, and you realize you're thirsty. That's no problem, though. The streets are lined with small delis and restaurants.

You come to a place called The Big Belly Deli and decide to go in. The name reminds you of a friend of yours after he eats too much food. He's a member of the Scooby Gang, and his name is . . .

"Shaggy!" you cry as you walk inside. You can't believe it! Shaggy, Scooby-Doo, Velma,

Fred, and Daphne are there, sitting at a shiny silver table.

"Hey, like, look who's here," Shaggy says. "Have a seat, old pal."

You fold up your scooter, take off your helmet, and sit down. A waiter is already taking the gang's order.

"I'll have an Empire State Building with extra mustard," Shaggy tells her.

You raise an eyebrow. You knew Shaggy had a big appetite, but could he really eat the Empire State Building?

Velma sees your expression and laughs. "The food here is named after tourist attractions in New York. I'm getting a Statue of Liberty," she says. "Shaggy wasn't really ordering the Empire State Building, although it might have seemed like he was."

"Things aren't often what they seem to be," Fred says. "We learned that lesson this weekend."

Velma takes a notebook out of her purse. "Fred's talking about a mystery we solved a few days ago," she explains. "Would you like to try to solve the case yourself? The notes on it are in this notebook, our Clue Keeper."

You should have known the gang had bumped into another mystery. You nod your head, ready for the challenge.

Velma hands you the Clue Keeper.

"We spent this weekend at the toy convention," she says. "I wrote all about it in here."

"You should be able to find a suspect

or a clue in most of the entries," Daphne adds. "We made it easy by adding symbols. The 👁👁 symbol means we found a suspect. And a 🔑 symbol means we found a clue."

Velma digs into her purse again. She hands you a pencil. "You'll need to write some things down as you go. At the end of each entry, we wrote some questions to help you organize the clues and suspects you find."

You open the Clue Keeper to the first entry. Can you solve this mystery?

There's only one way to find out.

You open the Clue Keeper and begin to read *The Case of the Living Doll.*

Clue Keeper Entry 1

"Like, Velma, when do we get to meet your cousin Elmer?" Shaggy asked me.

"I'm looking for him," I replied. I scanned the main hall of the Harrison Hotel.

I hadn't seen Elmer since we were kids. I had been busy solving mysteries with the Scooby gang. And Elmer was busy becoming a big-time toy inventor.

But a week earlier, he had e-mailed me to let me know he would be at the National Toy Convention in New York City. The gang and I thought it sounded like fun.

Finding Elmer in the crowd wouldn't be

easy. Toy inventors were displaying their newly created toys at booths. Model airplanes whizzed through the air. Electronic cars zipped along the floor. The hall was crowded with people trying out the toys.

Daphne was playing with a hula hoop. "I used to be hula hoop champ at summer camp," she said.

Scooby whizzed past me on roller skates, and Fred couldn't take his eyes off a miniature train set. The tracks wound all around the room.

"How come you're not playing with anything, Shaggy?" I asked.

Then I noticed Shaggy was eating an ice cream cone. "Like, I will, once I finish this free ice cream," Shaggy said.

"*Ook! Ook! Ook!*"

"What did you say, Shaggy?" I asked.

"That wasn't me," Shaggy said. We both looked down. A tiny monkey was pulling his pant leg. "Hey, little guy," Shaggy greeted him.

The monkey climbed up Shaggy's leg and hopped onto his shoulder. Then it grabbed the ice cream away from Shaggy.

"Hey!" Shaggy complained.

"Bananas! There you are!" a voice cried.

I turned around. The voice belonged to my cousin Elmer! Some people say we look alike. Elmer has short, brown hair and glasses. He wore an orange sweater and red pants.

"Velma!" Elmer cried. He gave me a hug. "I'm so glad you could make it."

Bananas scooped up some ice cream and threw it on the floor.

Shaggy cleared his throat. "*Ahem*. Could you do something about this ice-cream-stealing guy on my shoulder?"

"Of course," Elmer said. He held out his arm, and Bananas hopped on.

Something about that monkey wasn't quite right. Then I knew what it was.

"Gosh, Elmer," I said. "Is Bananas your latest invention?"

Elmer beamed with pride. "That's right. Bananas is an electronic monkey. I'm officially unveiling Bananas at the convention in two days. If I get a contract from a big toy company, I can make millions of Bananas and sell them in stores everywhere."

"Electronic? You mean, Bananas is a toy? He's not real?" Shaggy looked amazed.

"That's right," Elmer said.

"I think you've got a hit on your hands," I said. "Bananas is really cute."

"I hope so," Elmer said. "Listen, Bananas and I have to get some sleep. We have a big day tomorrow. How about I meet you and your friends for breakfast in the morning? I'm staying right here in the hotel. Are you?"

"Yes, we are. Breakfast sounds great," I said. I waved to Elmer as he walked off with Bananas.

Crash! Shaggy and I turned toward the sound. We saw that Scooby had rolled into a woman.

Shaggy and I rushed to help her.

"*Rorry,*" Scooby said.

The woman smoothed out her dress. She patted her hair. "That's okay," she said. "This convention couldn't get any worse, anyway."

"Like, this place is so much fun!" Shaggy said. "What's the matter?"

The woman sighed. "My name is Mary

Andrews," she said. "I make dolls. Good old-fashioned dolls. But all anyone wants these days is electronic toys. They're pieces of junk, if you ask me." 👁️👁️

"I think they're kind of fun," Shaggy said.

"Of course. Everyone does," said Mary Andrews sadly. "If you'll excuse me."

Mary Andrews left the room. Shaggy, Scooby, and I went to find Daphne and Fred. They were playing a new video game. Together, we explored the hall for a while longer, and then we checked into our rooms.

Daphne and I shared a room. Fred, Shaggy, and Scooby had the room next door.

"I sure am beat," I told Daphne as I un-packed my things. "I could use a good night's sleep. Tomorrow, I want to see more of what Elmer and Bananas can do."

I was about to shut off the light when there was a loud knock on the door. I got out of bed and peered through the peephole.

It was Elmer!

And he looked terrible!

I opened the door and Elmer rushed in. "Velma, the worst thing has happened!" he cried. "Someone has stolen Bananas!"

"**D**id you catch the 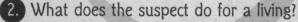 on page 10? I thought you would. We've found our first suspect. Answer these questions about this suspect in your Clue Keeper notebook."

 1. What is the suspect's name?

2. What does the suspect do for a living?

3. Why might the suspect want to steal Bananas?

Clue Keeper Entry 2

Daphne dressed, then ran and got Fred, Shaggy, and Scooby. After I changed, we met in the hall and, together, followed Elmer to his hotel room.

There was a single bed in the room. The covers were tossed aside. It looked like Elmer had sprung out of bed in a hurry. At the foot of the bed was a tiny bed with the word BANANAS written on it. The tiny bed was empty.

"Are you sure Bananas isn't in here somewhere?" I asked Elmer.

"Like, maybe Bananas wasn't sleepy," Shaggy suggested. "When I can't sleep, I like to grab a midnight snack."

Elmer shook his head. "No. He's been stolen. I know he has."

"How can you be so sure?" asked Fred. "Did you hear or see anything?"

Elmer looked like he was about to speak when somebody knocked on the open door.

I turned. A woman in a bathrobe stood in the doorway. An electronic duck waddled at her feet.

Scooby-Doo sniffed the duck.

"*Rello*," said Scooby.

"*Quack!*" replied the duck in a mechanical voice. Scooby jumped back.

"Elmer, what's going on here? You're making such a racket!" the woman asked crossly. She looked at Scooby with narrowed eyes. "I didn't know they allowed dogs in this hotel."

"Well, I didn't know they let ducks in here, either," Shaggy said.

"Quacky isn't a real duck," said the

woman. She picked up the toy duck. "Quacky is my latest invention."

"This is Benita Booker, a fellow toy inventor," Elmer explained. Then Elmer introduced me and the rest of the gang.

"My room is right next door," Benita said. "You and your noisy friends woke me up from a sound sleep."

Elmer turned to Benita. "I'm sorry. It's just that . . ." His voice choked. "Bananas is missing!"

I thought I detected a thin smile on Benita's face. "Oh, dear," said Benita. "I hope you find him."

"Thank you, Benita," said Elmer.

"I'd better get back to sleep," Benita said. "It looks like Quacky and I will have a big day tomorrow."

"*Quack!*" said Quacky.

Benita and Quacky left and Elmer closed the door. "Elmer, you were about to tell us what happened to Bananas," I reminded him.

"Oh, yes," said Elmer. "Well, I put Bananas to sleep in his bed. Then I read him a book about his favorite character — Curious George."

"Good choice!" said Shaggy.

Elmer nodded. "Then I fell asleep. But I must have heard a noise, because when I woke up, Bananas's bed was empty. I jumped up — and then I saw it!"

"Saw what?" I asked.

Elmer took a deep breath. "It was — a doll. I mean, it looked like a doll, but it was alive. It had blond curls. And its blue eyes seemed to look right through me. It was carrying Bananas."

16

"Are you talking about an electronic toy, like Bananas and Quacky?" Daphne asked.

"I'm not sure," Elmer replied. "It didn't look electronic. It looked like an old-fashioned doll had come to life. It was so creepy!" he shuddered.

"Did you try to catch it?" Fred asked.

Elmer nodded. "I did. But I tripped over Bananas's bed. When I got back up, the doll had vanished. And so had Bananas!" Elmer looked like he was going to cry.

"Don't worry," I told Elmer. "The Scooby gang is on the case. We'll get to the bottom of this, won't we, guys?"

"*Rou–bet!*" said Scooby.

Shaggy and Scooby's Mystery-Solving Tips

"Zoinks! Did you see the on page 15. They point to a suspect in the entry. Answer these questions in your Clue Keeper while Scooby and I go grab ourselves a snack. (Solving mysteries always makes us hungry!)"

1. What is the suspect's name?

2. What does the suspect do for a living?

3. Why might the suspect want to steal Bananas?

19

Clue Keeper Entry 3

Early the next morning we met Elmer in the hotel dining room. He looked like he hadn't slept at all. He nervously jabbed at his plate of waffles.

"Don't worry, Elmer," Daphne said soothingly. "We'll find out who took Bananas."

"I know who took Bananas!" Elmer said loudly. Then he leaned over and spoke in a harsh whisper. "It was that doll. That living doll."

"We believe you," I said. "But it can't hurt to think of people who might have wanted to steal Bananas."

Fred gazed around the dining room. Benita Booker and Quacky sat at a nearby table. Men and women in business suits were gathered around her. "I think Benita is a possible suspect," Fred said. "She seems happy now that Bananas is out of the way."

"That's silly," Elmer said. "There's room in this business for both Quacky and Bananas. Besides, Quacky can't do nearly as much as Bananas. He just waddles around and quacks."

"Elmer, can you think of anyone else at all who might want to see you fail at this show?" I asked.

Elmer thought for a minute. Then his eyes widened.

"Of course!" Elmer said. "Tyler Childs. It's got to be Tyler."

"Who's that?" Daphne asked.

"Tyler and I were partners," Elmer explained. "At least, that's how we started out. I ended up doing all the work. So I went out on my own and created Bananas. Tyler's started his own toy business, but he's been jealous of me ever since."

That sounded like a good lead to me. "Is he here at the show?"

Elmer nodded. "He's right over there," he said. He pointed to a table in the corner. A tall man with blond hair sat by himself. His expression was unhappy.

Fred stood. "Let's split up, gang," he said. "Daphne and I will talk to Benita. Shaggy and Scooby, see if you can find Mary Andrews, the woman with the old-fashioned dolls. And Velma, why don't you have a talk with Tyler Childs?"

"No problem," I said.

Elmer seemed relieved to see that we were taking action. He decided to go off on his own and search for Bananas.

I walked over to Tyler Childs. "Hello, I'm Velma Dinkley," I said. "Elmer Dinkley's cousin. Nice to meet you."

The dark look on Tyler's face got even darker.

"I wish I could say the same," Tyler said. "But any cousin of Elmer's is no friend of mine. Why did you come over here? Just so you could brag about how great Bananas is?"

Boy, this guy had an attitude. "Actually, I have bad news about Bananas," I said. "He's been stolen."

Tyler raised an eyebrow. Then he broke into a big smile.

Daphne's Mystery-Solving Tips

"Gosh! Velma's cousin Elmer is pretty upset, isn't he? I hope we solve this mystery soon. We've been doing a pretty good job finding suspects. We found one more. Did you see the on page 22? Answer these questions about our third suspect."

1. What is the suspect's name?

2. How does the suspect know Elmer Dinkley?

3. Why might the suspect want to steal Bananas?

24

Clue Keeper Entry 4

"That's the best news I've heard all year!" he said. "I guess that leaves Elmer with nothing. Ha!"

"You seem pretty happy about it," I said. "I guess you're happy for Benita Booker, too? Now her Quacky is the star of the convention."

Tyler scowled. "Of course not! Benita is my competition, too."

I needed more information. "Do you mind telling me where you were last night?" I asked him.

Tyler raised an eyebrow. "Oh, I get it. You

must be that mystery-solving cousin Elmer always talked about." He shrugged. "I have nothing to hide. I went to see a late movie last night. *The Creature That Ate Milwaukee.*"

"Thanks," I said.

I wasn't sure if I believed Tyler Childs. But I knew one thing for sure. I *was* going to keep my eye on him until this case was solved!

The dining room was emptying as I left Tyler Childs. I found Daphne and Fred waiting for me by the doorway. I told them about Tyler and his bad attitude.

"We should definitely keep an eye on that guy," Fred agreed.

It was my turn to frown. "Elmer could be making big deals, too. But he won't be able to do anything unless we find Bananas."

Daphne put a hand on my shoulder. "I'm sure we'll get some more leads. Maybe Shaggy and Scooby found out something from Mary Andrews."

We all walked into the hallway. I looked around. "I wonder where they are."

Although we didn't know it then (Shaggy and Scooby-Doo told us everything later), they were busy having quite an adventure.

While we were interviewing our suspects, Shaggy and Scooby went back to the main hall. They thought they might find Mary Andrews there. They were right. She was at a table, showing off her dolls.

Mary told Shaggy and Scooby that she

was up late last night sewing doll clothes. She didn't know anything about Bananas.

It wasn't much of an alibi. But Shaggy and Scooby didn't have anything else to go on. They got on the nearest elevator and headed back down to meet us.

Shaggy pressed a button. The elevator doors closed.

Nothing happened.

"That's weird," Shaggy said. He pressed the buttons until they all lit up. "Like, we're not going anywhere."

Then they heard a soft sound behind them. It sounded like the pattering of tiny feet.

Shaggy and Scooby looked at each other.

"Did you hear that, Scoob?"

Scooby nodded.

Shaggy gulped. "I was afraid of that. I thought we were the only ones here."

Shaggy and Scooby slowly turned around. Behind them was a doll. The doll had curly blond hair. It wore a dress. And it had a strange smile on its face.

"Leave the hotel now," said the doll in a

creepy, high-pitched voice. "Or dolly will get you!"

Just then, the elevator door opened. Scooby and Shaggy ran out of there. And the doll ran right after them!

Clue Keeper Entry 5

Scooby and Shaggy met us in the hall. They ran right into us, in fact, knocking us all down in a heap.

"What's going on?" Fred asked them. That's when they told us all about the creepy doll in the elevator. We looked around, but didn't see any sign of her.

"So you didn't see what happened to the doll?" I asked.

Shaggy and Scooby hugged each other. The rest of us got to our feet. "I don't care if I ever see that doll again!" Shaggy said.

"Like, that thing was creepy. Dolls are supposed to be cute and cuddly. They're not supposed to chase you."

"But how scary can a little doll be?" Daphne asked.

"Don't you know anything? Dolls are way scary!" said a voice.

I turned around. It was Tyler Childs. He must have overheard us.

"What do you mean?" I asked.

"Haven't you ever seen *Revenge of the Doll*? Or *Revenge of the Doll 2*?" he asked.

We shook our heads.

Tyler rolled his eyes. "They're only two of the greatest horror movies ever made. You see, dolls look innocent. But they're small. They can get into places people can't. That's the beauty of it. You think everything's fine, and then, *blammo!* The doll's got you."

"*Rammo!*" Scooby said, shuddering.

"What's all this about scary dolls, anyway?" Tyler asked.

I looked Tyler right in the eye. "Why don't you tell us?" I asked him.

Tyler shrugged. "Whatever. Good luck solving your little mystery." He walked off, disappearing around a corner.

"You sure were right about him," Fred said under his breath.

"And *he* sure knows a lot about dolls," Daphne added.

I mulled over Shaggy's story. "He's not the only one who knows about dolls. I'd like to question Mary Andrews, myself."

Then I heard Mary's voice behind me.

"Oh, there you all are!" she said.

"Wow, our suspects are coming right to us," Daphne whispered to me. "Is that lucky, or what?"

Mary stopped in front of me. "Are you Elmer Dinkley's cousin?" she asked.

"That's right. Velma Dinkley," I said.

"I was wondering if you could help me," Mary said. "You see, there's a rumor going around that you're helping Elmer find his lost Bananas. Well, I'm missing something, too!"

"One of your dolls?" Daphne asked.

Mary nodded. "One of my best pieces. I went to unpack her this morning — and the box was empty!"

"So your doll was stolen last night?" I asked.

Mary looked thoughtful. "Maybe," she said. "But maybe not. I checked into this hotel three days ago. It could have happened anytime since then."

"We'll help you," Fred said.

"Why, isn't she a suspect?" Shaggy whispered to me.

"She still is," I whispered back. "She might be trying to throw us off the trail."

"Ms. Andrews, if we're going to find your doll, we'll need to know what it looks like," said Daphne.

Mary Andrews nodded. She reached into her purse and pulled out a photo.

"This is her," she said. "My sweet little Cindy."

We looked at the photo. The doll had curly blond hair. Blue eyes. She wore a frilly dress.

"Zoinks!" Shaggy shouted. "Like, that's the doll that tried to attack us!"

Velma's Mystery-Solving Tips

"**J**inkies! A lot's happened in this entry. First Tyler gave us a lecture on creepy dolls. Then Mary Andrews came to us for help. We also found an important clue. Did you see the 🔦 on page 34? Answer the questions here to help you figure out what's happening."

1 What is the clue?

2. What does it have to do with the theft of Bananas?

3. Which suspect could be responsible for this clue?

35

Clue Keeper Entry # 6

Mary Andrews looked confused. "Little Cindy attacked you? What are you talking about?"

"We'll explain everything, Ms. Andrews," Daphne said.

"I think we need to examine that elevator," I said. "Shaggy and Scooby, you come with me."

Shaggy folded his arms across his chest. "No way!" Shaggy said. "Scooby and I aren't going back there again. Are we, Scoob?"

"*Ro-way!*" Scooby agreed.

But we had to retrace their steps if we

were going to find any clues. I had to con-vince them to help. Luckily, I had an idea.

"We'll take the elevator back to the main hall, where you first met Mary," I said. "I hear they're giving away free cotton candy today."

"*Rotten randy!*" said Scooby, wagging his tail.

"Like, it's not rotten candy, Scoob, it's de-licious!" Shaggy said. "All right, Velma. We'll go with you."

We left Fred and Daphne talking with Ms. Andrews. Shaggy and Scooby led me down the hallway, to the elevator.

The elevator door opened. A few people got off, and we stepped into the empty eleva-tor car.

Shaggy shivered. "This is where it hap-pened, all right. That doll just appeared!"

I looked up. A vent on the ceiling led the way to the elevator shaft above. "Maybe it dropped in from up there."

"Maybe," Shaggy said. "But that doesn't explain how a doll walks and talks all by it-self!"

Then I noticed something on the floor, in the corner: a small jumble of colored wire. Just like the kind that attaches to electronic panels.

I picked up the wires. "I think I have some idea, Shaggy," I said.

Bing! The elevator stopped.

"Thank goodness!" Shaggy said. "It's cotton candy time!"

The door opened. But we weren't on the same floor as the convention hall.

The hallway in front of us was dark.

"Like, where are we?" Shaggy asked.

"There's only one way to find out," I said. I stepped out into the hallway. Shaggy and Scooby didn't want to be alone in the elevator, so they followed me. The elevator doors closed behind them.

I shone my flashlight down the dimly lit hall. "It looks like we went down to the basement instead of up to the main hall," I said.

And then I heard it.

First there was a clatter. Then there was a noise, like something rolling.

Hundreds of marbles were rolling on the floor toward us.

"Shaggy, Scooby, jump out of the way!" I called out as I tried to leap to the side. I wasn't fast enough. My feet slid on the marbles.

And my warning came too late. Shaggy and Scooby slipped on the marbles and fell. I fell, too — and dropped my flashlight.

"Are you all right?" I asked Shaggy and Scooby.

"We're okay," Shaggy said. "But what was that all about?"

Suddenly, we heard another sound.

A giggle.

My flashlight shone in the direction of the noise. Then I gasped.

The light lit up a tiny doll's face. Its blue eyes seemed to stare right at us.

"Zoinks! It's the living doll!" Shaggy cried.

"Leave the hotel now," chanted Little Cindy. "Noooowww!!!"

"**V**elma, Shaggy, and Scooby are in a tight spot! We'll find out how they get out of it in the next entry. First, see if you can find the clue in this entry. Look for the ⚲ . Then answer these questions."

1. What is the clue?

2. What does the clue tell you about the living doll?

3. Which suspects might have left this clue?

42

Clue Keeper Entry #7

Just in time, the elevator door opened. Shaggy and Scooby ran into it. I wanted to stay and get a closer look at the doll, but they pulled me in.

"We saved you, Velma," Shaggy said.

"Thanks, guys," I said. "Why don't you get that cotton candy? There's something I want to check out."

Shaggy and Scooby got out by the main hall. I returned to where I had left Daphne and Fred. I told them about our basement encounter with the living doll. Then I showed them the wires I had found.

"Very interesting," said Fred.

"You can say that again," agreed Daphne. "But one thing's still bugging me. How did that doll get into Elmer's room to steal Bananas?"

"That's just what I was wondering," I said. There was only one way to find out. We headed up to Elmer's room.

We found Elmer sitting on a chair, staring at Bananas's empty bed. He looked up when we came in.

"Have you found him?" Elmer asked. "Have you found Bananas?"

"Not yet," I said. "But we're getting close."

Elmer slumped back in his chair. "It's no use. I'm supposed to present Bananas to the toy convention first thing tomorrow morning. It looks like all my hard work was for nothing."

"Maybe not," Fred said. "We just need to check out a few more things. For instance, your door was open just now. Was it open the night Bananas was stolen?"

Elmer shook his head. "No. I remember I was very careful. I even locked the chain lock. I didn't want anything to happen to Bananas."

I looked around the room. "There must be some way the doll could have gotten in. We just missed it last time."

Daphne walked to the window, lifted it, and looked out. "It's too high up. And the ledge is too narrow. I don't think a doll could walk across it. Not even a living doll!"

Fred stood on a chair. An air vent was screwed into the wall. "The doll might have

come through here," he said. "But then the vent wouldn't be screwed in like this."

There had to be something.

I noticed that there was a door on the wall opposite Elmer's bed.

"This door leads to the next room," I said. "Some hotels use them in case people request adjoining rooms."

"But those doors are always locked," Fred said. "This one's even got an electric lock. You need a special code to open it."

I turned the handle. The door creaked.

Then it opened.

"It looks like someone figured out the code," I said. "Someone with a knowledge of electronics."

I closed the door.

"Wait!" Elmer cried. "That door could lead to Bananas!"

"That door definitely leads to a suspect," I said. "But I don't think Bananas is here. If we want to rescue Bananas, we have to do one thing."

I looked at Fred.

Fred nodded. "We need a plan!"

"Dish yoush fish – whoops! I forgot to swallow my cotton candy. What I meant to say was, did you find the in this entry? We're really close to finding Bananas now. Answer the clue questions to see how close you are to figuring things out."

1. What is the clue?

2. How did the suspect use the clue to steal Bananas?

3. Which suspect does this clue point to?

47

Clue Keeper Entry #8

With Elmer's help, we began phase one of our plan that night. Elmer made an announcement in the convention hall. "As you know, Bananas, my electronic monkey, has been stolen," Elmer told the crowd through a microphone.

The toy inventors nodded their heads.

"I was supposed to unveil Bananas tomorrow morning," Elmer continued. "Well, I don't want to disappoint you. So I'm going to unveil my biggest, best invention yet!"

There was a murmur in the crowd. I saw

Benita Booker and Tyler Childs step closer to Elmer. Both looked very curious.

Elmer looked at me nervously. I nodded at him to go on.

"Tomorrow morning, I will reveal . . . life-size electronic action figures!" Elmer said.

The crowed oohed and ahhed.

"I've been keeping them hidden in a special storeroom in the basement," Elmer said. "But tomorrow, you'll all get to see them."

Elmer put down the microphone and walked down to us.

"How'd I do?" he asked.

"Terrific!" Daphne said.

"Yeah, like I can't wait to see those life-size action figures," Shaggy said. "They sound cool."

Daphne, Fred, and I looked at Shaggy and Scooby. They took a step back as they realized what we had in mind.

"No way," Shaggy said. "Scoob and I aren't going to pretend to be toys. That doll is one toy I don't want to play with!"

"*Right!*" agreed Scooby.

49

"Come on, Scooby," Daphne said. "Would you do it for a Scooby Snack?"

"*Ro.*" Scooby closed his eyes and folded his arms.

"How about two Scooby Snacks?" I asked.

"*Ro.*" Scooby wouldn't budge. Then he opened one eye. "*Rhee?*"

I smiled. "Okay, Scooby. Three Scooby Snacks!"

Shaggy sighed. "I guess you can count me in, too."

Now it was time for phase two of the plan. The hotel had agreed to let us use an empty storage room in the basement.

We disguised Shaggy and Scooby as action figures. We put a superhero's cape around Scooby's neck. We gave a helmet and shield to Shaggy.

We set up Shaggy and Scooby in the storeroom. Elmer helped them pose in action-figure poses. Shaggy stood and looked brave. Scooby had one hand on his hip, and the other raised in a greeting.

"Great," Elmer said. "You guys look per-
fect."

"Like, how long do we have to stay this
way?" Shaggy asked. "I have an itch on my
nose."

"Don't worry," I said. "I don't think we'll
have to wait too long for our suspect to take
the bait."

Daphne and Fred left to hide out in the
hallway. Elmer and I hid behind a wide
wooden crate in the room with Shaggy and
Scooby.

I could see Shaggy was having a hard time staying still. He kept twitching his nose.

The storeroom was dark and dusty. My nose started to itch, too.

Shaggy looked like he couldn't take it anymore. I was sure he was going to sneeze. . . .

And then the door creaked open. A tiny figure walked through the door.

The Living Doll!

Little Cindy had a screwdriver in her hand.

"I'll take you apart," said the doll. This time, her voice sounded deeper. "Elmer will not ruin things for me!"

Shaggy and Scooby-Doo sprang into action.

Scooby jumped in front of the doll. "Well, hello, dolly!" Shaggy said, grabbing at her. Little Cindy darted around Scooby and quickly ran out of the room.

"Follow her!" Elmer yelled.

We ran down the hall after the doll. She disappeared into another storeroom.

This room was dark, too, but I could make out a box in the center of it. A blanket covered the box. I yanked the blanket away. The box turned out to be a wire cage. Inside sat a small monkey.

"Bananas!" Elmer yelled. He took a remote control from his pocket. He pushed a button, and Bananas started to jump up and down and chatter excitedly. Elmer quickly freed him from his cage.

Fred and Daphne ran in behind us. Fred spotted Little Cindy on the floor and scooped her up.

"I've got her!" Fred said. He opened a small door on Cindy's neck. I could see electric wires and a panel inside.

"Just as we thought," Daphne said. "Someone has altered the doll so it can be controlled electronically."

"And whoever's controlling her has got to be nearby," I said.

Just then, a dark figure ran past the door. Whoever it was wore a dark, hooded cape.

"There goes our suspect!" Daphne cried.

Elmer had a determined look on his face. "I'll finish this, cousin," he told me. "Come on, Bananas!"

Elmer ran out of the room. The running figure was just ahead of him. Quick as lightning, Elmer took a real banana from his pocket, peeled it, and slid it down the hallway. The fleeing suspect fell to the floor with a thud. "Nice job, cuz," I complimented Elmer as we rushed to see our suspect.

"Now it's time for me to find out who stole Bananas," Fred said.

"**A**ll right! Our food is here," Shaggy cheers.

The waitress plops a big bowl of salad in front of you. "Here's your Central Park," she says.

You put down the Clue Keeper. You can't eat now! You're too excited. Velma notices that you're not starting your salad. "You look like you're about to solve the mystery," she says. "You can do it. First, take a look at the three suspects we found."

"Then, think about the clues," Daphne adds. "Ask yourself which suspect could have left all three clues."

Fred swallows a french fry. "Good luck," he says.

Turn the page to discover if you solved The Case of the Living Doll correctly.

"It was Benita Booker!" Fred says. "With Bananas gone, her electronic duck, Quacky, would be the star of the show."

"The clues all pointed to Benita," says Velma, between bites of her sandwich. "First, we found out that Mary Andrews was missing a doll. That told us that we were dealing with a real doll and not some kind of supernatural creature."

"Mary Andrews might have used the doll on her own," Daphne says. "But then Velma found the electronic wires in the elevator.

Mary didn't know anything about making electronic toys."

Velma takes a sip of water. "I didn't like Tyler much. But the fact that Bananas was stolen didn't benefit him."

"We knew for sure it was Benita when Velma realized that the door inside Elmer's room was unlocked," says Fred. "Benita would have had the know-how to break the electronic code."

"I had a hunch Benita was hiding Bananas in the basement," Velma said. "After all, we did encounter the doll down there. And I knew she couldn't resist trying to ruin Elmer's chance at success again. That's why our plan worked so well."

"I'm glad everything worked out all right for Elmer," Shaggy says. "Bananas was the star of the show!"

"*Rooby-rooby-roo!*" Scooby cheers.